GROLIER
BOOK CLUB EDITION

WALT DISNEY'S

Brer Rabbit
Saves His Skin

Brer Fox and Brer Bear were
always watching Brer Rabbit.

They knew that Brer Rabbit
was full of tricks.

One day Brer Rabbit was looking
for a cool place to take a nap.
He came to a well.
A bucket was hanging at the top.

"That bucket looks like a cool place," thought Brer Rabbit.

Brer Fox was watching him.

"That rabbit is up to something," thought Brer Fox.

Brer Rabbit jumped
into the bucket.

The bucket dropped into the well.
Brer Rabbit was surprised.

There was another bucket
at the bottom of the well.
   As Brer Rabbit went down,
the other bucket came up.
   Brer Rabbit landed in
the water at the bottom
of the well.
   "How am I going to get
out of here?" he wondered.
   Brer Rabbit was trapped.

Brer Fox crept up to the well.

He peeked over the edge.

It was dark inside.
"Hey, Brer Rabbit,"
he called. "What are you
doing down there?"

When Brer Rabbit
saw Brer Fox, he
saw a way
to get out.

"I'm fishing,"
he said.

"Fishing?" cried Brer Fox.
"What kind of fish are down there?"

"Big ones!" said Brer Rabbit.

"I want to catch
some big fish, too,"
said Brer Fox.
"How do I get down?"

"It's easy,"
said Brer Rabbit.
"Just climb into
the bucket."

So Brer Fox climbed into the bucket
at the top of the well.

Brer Rabbit was light.
His bucket came up.

Brer Fox was heavy.
His bucket went down.

When Brer Fox got to the bottom,
he reached into the water.
    But he didn't catch any fish.
    That is no surprise.
    Fish live in fish ponds, not wells.

When Brer Rabbit got to the top,
he jumped out of the bucket.

"Some go up and some go down,"
he said.

And off he went to find a safer
napping place.

By and by he came to a hollow tree.
There was a hole at the top and
a hole at the bottom.

"That tree looks safe," he thought.

Just then Brer Bear came along.
He saw Brer Rabbit.
"That rabbit is up to something,"
thought Brer Bear.

Brer Rabbit crawled
through the bottom hole.

Brer Bear crept up to the tree.
"Brer Rabbit must be hiding
something in there," he thought.

Brer Rabbit lay down
to take his nap inside
the tree.

But when he looked up,
he was surprised.

The tree
was full of
honeycomb!

The honeycomb
was full of bees!

"This is no place
for a nap," thought
Brer Rabbit.
And he raced
out of the tree.

Brer Bear grabbed him by the ears.
"You can't fool me," said Brer Bear.
"What's inside that tree?"

"Honey," said Brer Rabbit.

"Honey?" cried Brer Bear. "I want some!"

"Help yourself," said Brer Rabbit.
"Just reach into that top hole."

Brer Bear let go of Brer Rabbit.
He reached into the hole
at the top of the tree.

He pulled out a piece of honeycomb.
It was dripping with honey.
"wow!" said Brer Bear.

But in a minute
his hand was buzzing with bees.
"yeow!" cried Brer Bear.

Brer Bear went running down the road.
The bees went buzzing after him.

Brer Rabbit laughed
and laughed.
"Trouble comes and
trouble goes," he said.

When the bees went away,
Brer Bear stopped running.
He was hot and thirsty.
He went to the well to get
a bucket of water.

Brer Bear turned the crank.
Up came a bucket of Brer Fox!

"Brer Rabbit tricked me," said Brer Fox.
"He tricked me, too," said Brer Bear.
"It must be time
to trick Brer Rabbit."

So Brer Fox and Brer Bear got
shovels and some very sticky syrup.
  "We are going to turn that tricky rabbit
into a sticky rabbit," said Brer Fox.

Brer Bear dug a big hole in the road.

Then he filled the hole with syrup.

"Brer Rabbit won't hop into this hole when he sees the syrup," said Brer Bear.
"You are right!" said Brer Fox.
"We must cover the syrup with straw."

So off they went to get some straw.

While they were gone,
Brer Rabbit came hopping
down the road.

HIPPITY-HOP.

LIPPITY-LOP.

Up he went . . .

. . . and down he came—
SMACKETY-PLOP—
right in that hole
full of syrup.

Brer Rabbit was the stickiest rabbit
you ever saw.

He was sticky from the tops of
his ears to the tips of his toes.

"How am I going to get
this stuff off," he wondered.

He rolled in a pile of leaves.

He rolled in a pile of twigs.

He even tried pine cones.

But the sticky syrup would not come off.
And everything stuck to it.

Brer Rabbit was furious.
He leaped into the air.
He waved his arms.
He kicked his feet.
He shook his head.

"OWWW-EEEE-KERRIMMY!" he cried.

Just then Brer Fox and Brer Bear
came back.

There by the road was the scariest
creature they had ever seen.

It was making a terrible noise.

"It's a wild beast!" they cried.

Brer Fox and Brer Bear were so scared,
they ran away.

The next day Brer Fox
and Brer Bear set a trap
to catch the wild beast.
Along came Brer Rabbit.

"You'll never catch that wild beast,"
said Brer Rabbit.
"That wild beast is me!"

He jumped up and down
and waved his hands.

When Brer Fox and Brer Bear heard what he said,
hey were very angry.
  They leaped forward to grab Brer Rabbit.

SNAP!

They landed in their own trap.

Brer Rabbit began to laugh.

"When you look for trouble," he said,
"you are sure to find it."